3 4028 06911 0469
HARRIS COUNTY PUBLIC LIBRARY

J 629.227 Dav
David, Jack
Cruisers

$20.00
ocn179837827
12/02/2008

Cruisers

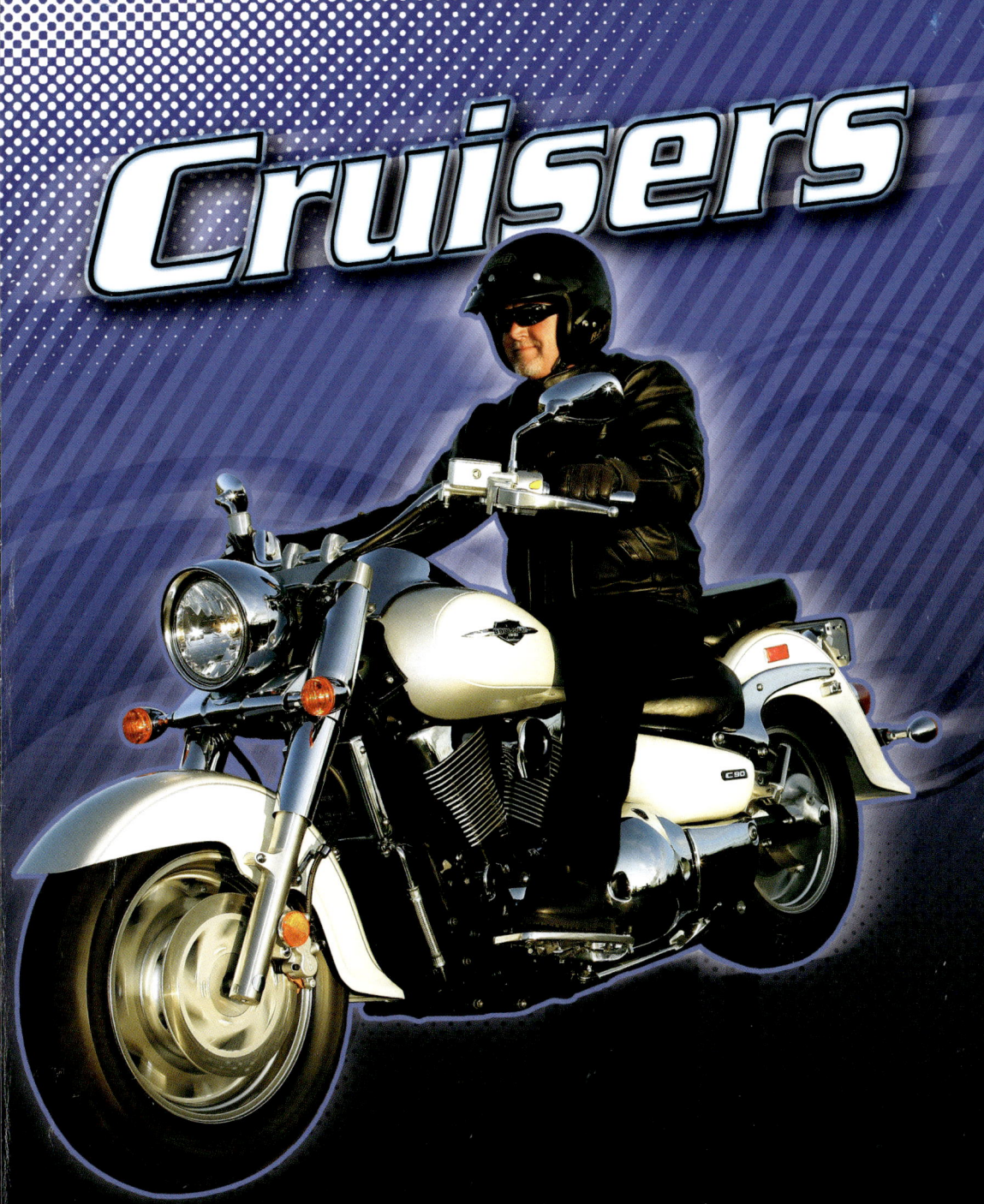

BY **JACK DAVID**

BELLWETHER MEDIA · MINNEAPOLIS, MN

Are you ready to take it to the extreme?
Torque books thrust you into the action-packed world of sports, vehicles, and adventure. These books may include dirt, smoke, fire, and dangerous stunts.
WARNING: read at your own risk.

Library of Congress Cataloging-in-Publication Data

David, Jack, 1968-
 Cruisers / by Jack David.
    p. cm. -- (Torque. Motorcycles)
 Includes bibliographical references and index.
 ISBN-13: 978-1-60014-132-4 (hbk. : alk. paper)
 ISBN-10: 1-60014-132-3 (hbk. : alk. paper)
 1. Motorcycles--Juvenile literature. 2. Motorcycle touring--Juvenile literature. I. Title.

TL440.15.D36 2008
629.227'5--dc22

2007014196

This edition first published in 2008 by Bellwether Media.

No part of this publication may be reproduced in whole or in part without written permission of the publisher. For information regarding permission, write to Bellwether Media Inc., Attention: Permissions Department, Post Office Box 1C, Minnetonka, MN 55345-9998.

Text copyright © 2008 by Bellwether Media.
SCHOLASTIC, CHILDREN'S PRESS, and associated logos are trademarks and/or registered trademarks of Scholastic Inc. Printed in the United States of America.

CONTENTS

CRUISERS IN ACTION	4
WHAT IS A CRUISER?	8
FEATURES	12
THE CRUISER EXPERIENCE	18
GLOSSARY	22
TO LEARN MORE	23
INDEX	24

CRUISERS IN ACTION

A man climbs onto his classic cruiser motorcycle. He puts on his helmet and starts the engine. He sits upright with his feet resting on the forward foot pegs. The big engine rumbles as he hits the road.

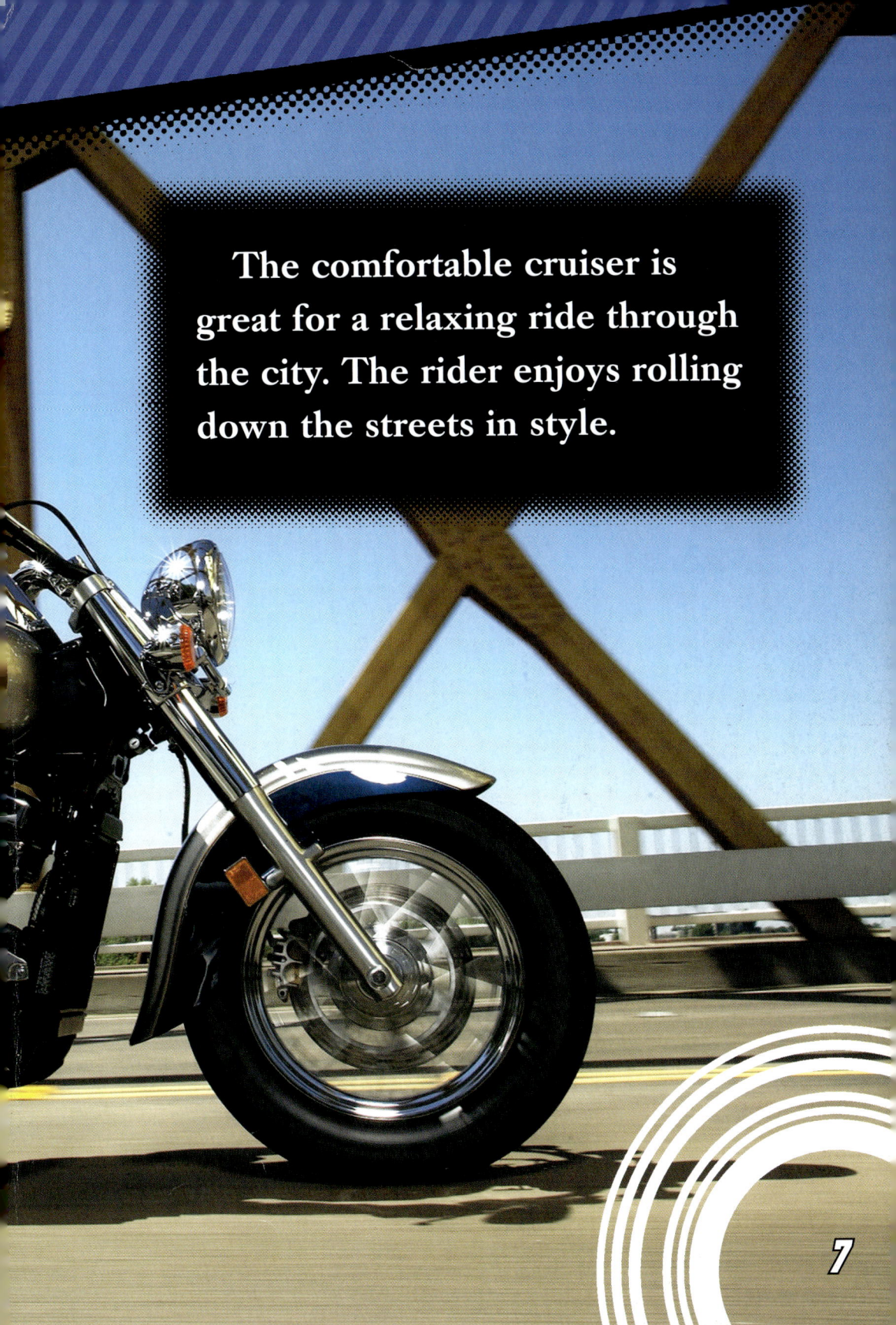

The comfortable cruiser is great for a relaxing ride through the city. The rider enjoys rolling down the streets in style.

WHAT IS A CRUISER?

Cruisers are based on the classic American motorcycles from the 1930s to the 1960s. They are built for comfort and style. They are not built to carry a lot of supplies. They are large bikes with powerful engines and comfortable seats.

FAST FACT
CRUISERS WERE MADE POPULAR BY AMERICAN MOVIE STARS IN THE 1950s.

Harley-Davidson, Polaris, Honda, Yamaha, and BMW make the most popular cruiser models. Cruisers are the best-selling style of motorcycle in the United States.

FEATURES

Cruisers are built for casual riding. Most of them have simple **V-twin** engines. This style of engine has two **cylinders** arranged in the shape of a V. They give cruisers their power and unique sound.

FAST FACT
CRUISERS WERE THE PRIMARY STYLE OF MOTORCYCLE USED BY THE UNITED STATES ARMY DURING WORLD WAR II.

Cruiser riders sit like cowboys sat on their horses in the old American west. Riders rest their feet on forward foot pegs and sit straight up or slightly leaned back. This riding position is even called "Western Saddle."

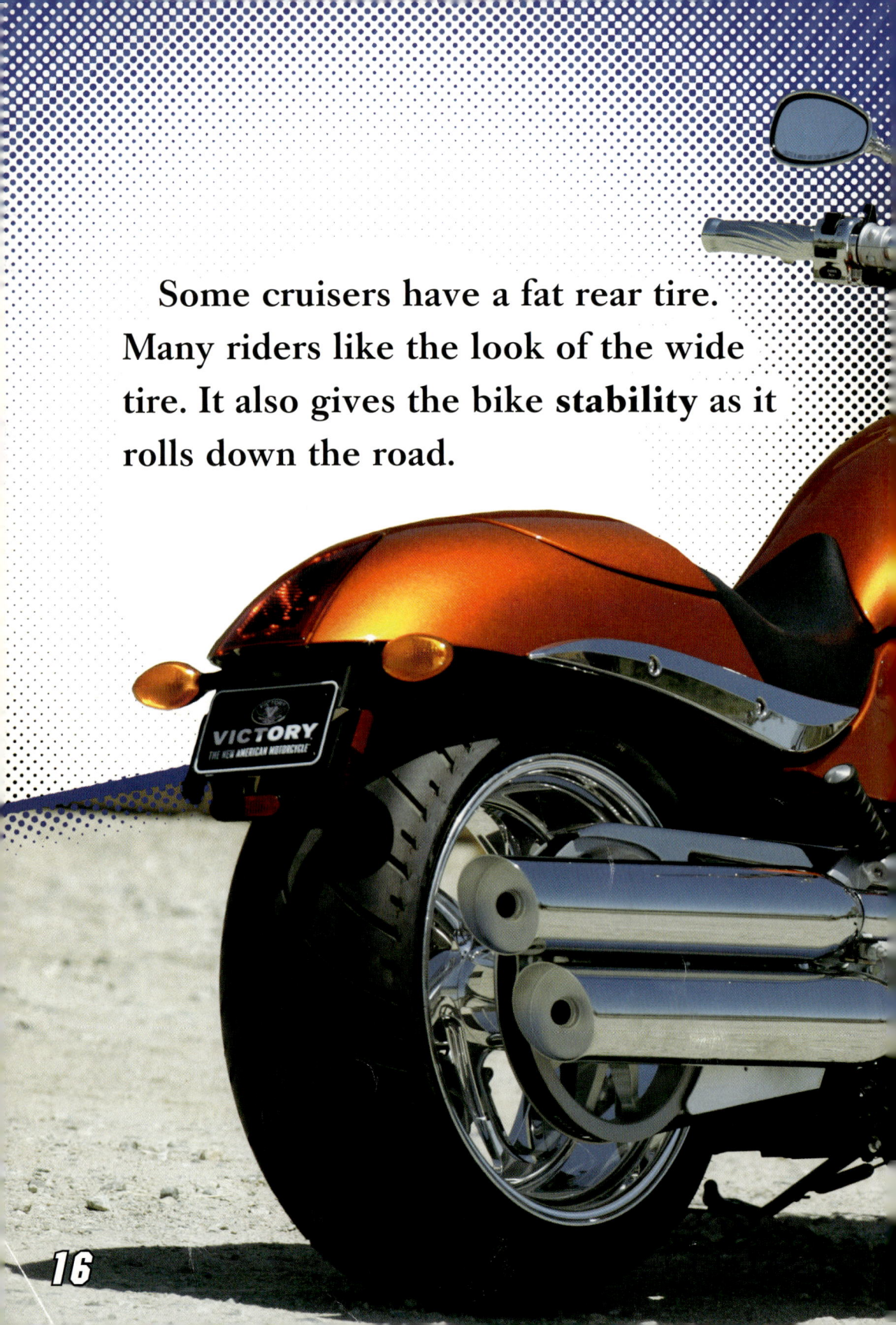

Some cruisers have a fat rear tire. Many riders like the look of the wide tire. It also gives the bike **stability** as it rolls down the road.

THE CRUISER EXPERIENCE

Cruiser riders often gather in large groups to admire each other's bikes and ride down the road. Most of their bikes do not have **fairings**. The drivers want to feel the wind on their faces as they ride.

FAST FACT
MANY OWNERS TURN CRUISERS INTO CHOPPERS. THIS STYLE OF CUSTOMIZED MOTORCYCLE INCLUDES HIGH HANDLEBARS AND A STRETCHED WHEELBASE.

Cruiser owners ride their comfortable bikes to relax. It doesn't matter if they're driving through a city or cruising on a highway. The laid-back riding style has made cruisers a favorite among riders.

GLOSSARY

cylinder–the engine part where fuel is burned to create power

fairing–the drag-reducing front panel of a motorcycle

stability–a property of sturdiness and control

v-twin–a type of motorcycle engine with two cylinders arranged in the shape of a V

Western Saddle–a riding style similar to how cowboys rode horses in the American west

TO LEARN MORE

AT THE LIBRARY

David, Jack. *Choppers*. Minneapolis, Minn.: Bellwether, 2007.

David, Jack. *Touring Motorcycles*. Minneapolis, Minn.: Bellwether, 2007.

Hill, Lee Sullivan. *Motorcycles*. Minneapolis, Minn.: Lerner Publications Co., 2004.

ON THE WEB

Learning more about motorcycles as easy as 1, 2, 3.

1. Go to www.factsurfer.com

2. Enter "motorcycles" into search box.

3. Click the "Surf" button and you will see a list of related web sites.

With factsurfer.com, finding more information is just a click away.

INDEX

1930s, 8
1950s, 10
1960s, 8
BMW, 11
choppers, 20
comfort, 7, 8, 21
cowboys, 15
cylinders, 12
engine, 4, 8, 12
fairings, 18
foot pegs, 4, 15
handlebars, 20
Harley-Davidson, 11
Honda, 11
movie stars, 10

Polaris, 11
stability, 16
United States, 11
United States Army, 14
V-twin engine, 12
Western Saddle, 15
World War II, 14
Yamaha, 11

The photographs in this book are reproduced through the courtesy of: American Suzuki Motor Corporation, cover, pp. 1, 4-5; Kawasaki Motors Corporation, pp. 6-7, 15, 21; Polaris Industries, pp. 8-9, 10-11, 12-13, 14 (bottom), 16-17; Yamaha Motor Corporation, pp. 14 (top), 18-19, 20 (top, bottom).

Harris County Public Library
Houston, Texas